This book belongs to

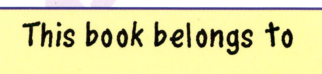

_____

_____

_____

Für Kerstin und Florian,
die Monster vom weißen Berg

tiger tales
an imprint of ME Media, LLC
202 Old Ridgefield Road, Wilton, CT 06897
First published in the United States 2002
Originally published in Germany 2000
by K. Thienemanns Verlag, Stuttgart, Vienna, Berne
Copyright ©2002 K. Thienemanns Verlag
English translation by Felix Kerntke
CIP Data is available
ISBN 1-58925-373-6
Printed in Hong Kong
All rights reserved
1 3 5 7 9 10 8 6 4 2

A Monster
Under
Alex's Bed

by Angelika Glitz

Illustrated by Imke Sönnichsen

tiger tales

A monster lives under Alex's bed. Although Alex has never seen it, he knows it's there, and he's sure it will squeeze through the space between the bed and the wall and steal his teddy bear.

Alex hears a noise. He quickly pulls his blanket over his head.

"Mommy!"

Alex's bedroom door opens. "Did you have a nightmare, Alex?" his mother asks.

"*Shh*," he whispers, "Quiet.
There's a monster under my bed."
Alex's mother laughs.
"Really," he says. "It made a very
scary noise."
Alex's mother runs her hands through
his hair. "Alright," she says. "Let's hear
that monster!"

Zoom!

"That's a passing car," says Alex's mother.
"I know," says Alex.

Rattle, rattle!

"That's only the wind in the blinds," his mother explains.

"Oh, everybody knows that," Alex replies.

Alex and his mother don't hear
any more noises.

"What's that shadow on the wall
over there?" Alex asks.

"That's only the tree outside
your window," says his mother,
smiling. That's what Alex
thinks, too. So he lays
back down in bed.

Alex's mother gives his nose a little kiss.
"Now go back to sleep," she says.
    "Like a big, sleeping monster," Alex says.

But Alex holds on to his mother's arm. And his mother can't leave with Alex holding her arm like that.

"Can't you check once more?" pleads Alex. "I mean, just so we can be really sure."

Alex's mother turns on her flashlight. She rolls the toy box out of the way. Then she slowly peeks underneath the bed.

"Wow," Alex thinks. "Mommy is so brave. The monster could get her any time."

"It's a mess under here!" his mother yells.
"Tomorrow you'll clean this up." Alex moans.
"And what about this old yogurt cup? And my
hat?" The cup and the hat fly out from under
the bed…

and then Alex's pants,
a toy camel,
a stuffed pig,
and . . .

Alex's mother sees two glowing eyes.

Aaaaaaaahhhhhhhh!

Alex's mother drops the flashlight. She jumps out from under the bed, grabs Alex, and rushes out of the room.

Slam! She closes the door.

Whoosh!

Push!

Crash!

Boing!

Oof!

Alex's mother piles up things in front of the door. The monster is trapped.

Alex's eyes glow. "Scary monster, isn't it? Hey, does it have five or seven heads? Does it have hair growing in its ears? Does it have bad breath?"

His mother trembles. She looks very pale. "Under your bed…" she whispers, "There's a mouse under your bed."

"A mouse?" says Alex. "What do you mean a mouse? A small, wimpy mouse?" Alex is really disappointed. "Can I pet it?" he asks.

"No way," say Alex's mother. "Mice are dangerous." Alex looks at his mother, annoyed. "You'd better sleep in my bed tonight," says Alex's mother.

Alex doesn't say a word. He usually
isn't allowed to sleep in his mother's bed.
"Tomorrow," he thinks, "I'll catch that mouse.
Then Mommy won't be scared anymore."

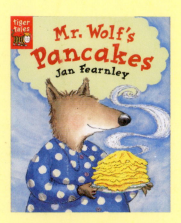

Mr. Wolf's Pancakes
by Jan Fearnley
ISBN 1-58925-354-X

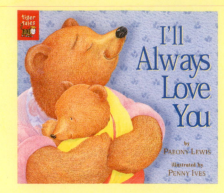

I'll Always Love You
by Paeony Lewis
illustrated by Penny Ives
ISBN 1-58925-360-4

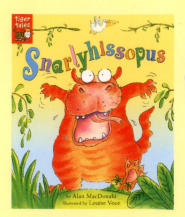

Snarlyhissopus
by Alan MacDonald
illustrated by Louise Voce
ISBN 1-58925-370-1

Explore the world of tiger tales!

More fun-filled and exciting stories await you!
Look for these paperback titles and more at your local
library or bookstore. And have fun reading!

tiger tales

202 Old Ridgefield Road, Wilton, CT 06897

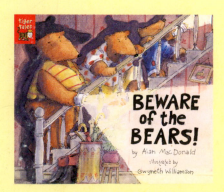

Beware of the Bears
by Alan MacDonald
illustrated by Gwyneth Williamson
ISBN 1-58925-359-0

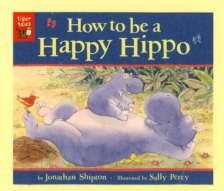

How to Be a Happy Hippo
by Jonathan Shipton
illustrated by Sally Percy
ISBN 1-58925-357-4

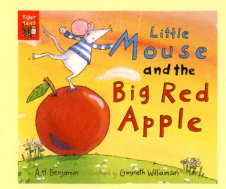

**Little Mouse
and the Big Red Apple**
by A.H. Benjamin
illustrated by Gwyneth Williamson
ISBN 1-58925-358-2